T0199068

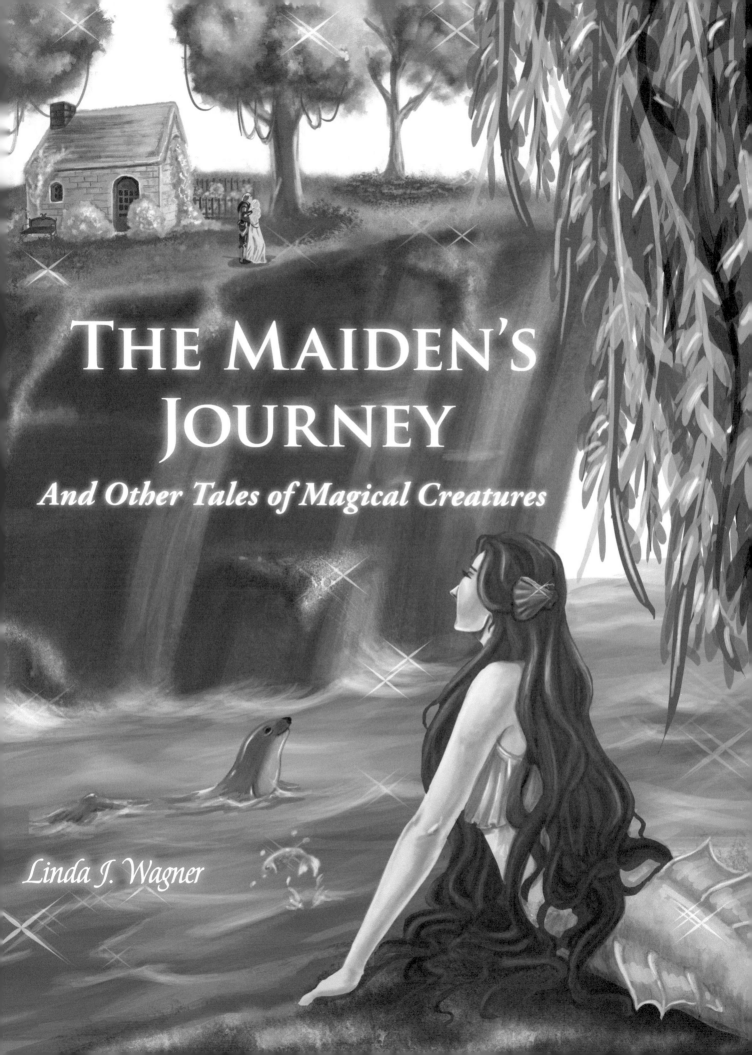

# THE MAIDEN'S JOURNEY

## And Other Tales of Magical Creatures

Linda J. Wagner

Balboa Press books may be ordered through booksellers or by contacting:

Balboa Press
A Division of Hay House
1663 Liberty Drive
Bloomington, IN 47403
www.balboapress.com
844-682-1282

ISBN: 978-1-5043-6913-8 (sc)
ISBN: 978-1-9822-6120-7 (hc)
ISBN: 978-1-5043-6912-1 (e)

Library of Congress Control Number: 2016920639

Print information available on the last page.

Balboa Press rev. date: 01/19/2021

BALBOA.PRESS
A DIVISION OF HAY HOUSE

For my son, Collin.

Thank you for sharing your wonder, creativity,
and poems for this book.

# The Maiden's Journey

"Because there are no impossible dreams…"

Linda J. Wagner

*Linda J. Wagner*

4

*Once upon a dream, in a village in the sea*
*There dwelt a mermaid maiden, of human heart was she*
*She secretly stole silent to spy a nearby cliff*
*And a tiny ivy cottage where human maidens lived*

*Perched at edge of jagged stone, defying surf and sound*
*The creatures of the deep blue sea caressed its banks around*
*In hopes of fleeting glances of ladies and their knights*
*'Tis told of a beauty sleeping and a maid of snow's pure white*

*Of a dancing maiden form, some do further tell*
*A lady of the mystical, the one they call Giselle*
*The tales of old told true, beyond the hills of gold*
*Rang echoes through the deepest depths of ancient Neptune's home*

*The maiden of the sea would come to splash at ocean's edge*
*Beneath a weeping willow tree, near the ivy cottage ledge*
*The willow tree stood tall and strong, sipping from a stream*
*Cradling like a lover, the mermaid while she dreamed*

*She dreamed of love and romance, though not the human kind*
*A love that dwells within the soul, entwining heart and mind*
*She often prayed to Neptune, the god of sea and love*
*To send her someone magical created from above*

*Someone so acquainted with magic and the art*
*Of serenading mermaids, to hypnotize their hearts*
*Perhaps the one may offer, "Dear Neptune, if you please!"*
*A mode of transportation, of pleasure and of ease*

*To reach the ivy cottage door secured with golden key*
*To enter into paradise, forever to be free*
*Appendages she craved, Phalanges! So divine*
*A sea nymph formed with dorsal fins eternally denied*

*One dark night the stars came out to splash the moonlit sky*
*The creatures of the sea and land could hear the mermaid cry*
*Her pounding heart was terrorized as lightning crashed the air*
*Poseidon challenged Neptune with warning and a dare*

*Commanding power o'er all the deep, he caused a violent storm*
*The silver stars escaped their doom, the willow wailed and mourned*
*To free the maiden from her curse of gripping weed of sea*
*Tangled in her mermaid's tale, who could set her free?*

*Somewhere in a prayer beyond the sea and night*
*A rescue was commissioned, an angel took to flight*
*Soaring through the cosmos, suspending time and space*
*Planetary checkpoints discovered not a trace*

*The mirror of creation enlightened with a glance*
*Revealed exact location of the master of song and dance*
*Armed with calm assurance, the one took rapid flight*
*To rescue the mermaid maiden from cruel and desperate plight*

12

The ligaments of sea life were quite beyond repair
So tenderest of transplants, he stitched with special care
Shimmering in sunlight, the stormy sky was cleared
The mermaid's tangled tendrils strangely disappeared

The tiny ivy cottage stood drenched and silently still
The master led the mermaid slowly up the hill
Like the maidens of the woods, the mermaid now transformed
Her destiny is altered, a soul has been reborn

Often while she slumbered beneath a slipper moon
The sound of someone singing would cause her heart to swoon
Nearby the weeping willow, the ocean and beyond
The maiden was enchanted with the master and his song

*Other Magical Tales...*

*The Swan Who Lived*

*I had a dream a swan was maimed*
*Her heart had broken in twain*
*Her wings were clipped by a hunter cruel*
*A ruthless rugged swain*

*The other swans were kind to her*
*They kept her in their care*
*She warned them of the hunter's cruel*
*And tempting evil lair*

*She knew that soon the time would come*
*For death to claim her soul*
*A crippled swan, how could she hope*
*To ever become whole?*

*One day soon a Prince of Blue*
*Happened across a sight*
*A swan at death alone in the brush*
*At the edge of a winter's night*

*Perplexed and sad, he could not pass*
*The creature was all alone*
*He started to dance and sing to her*
*A hopeful healing song*

*As she lie in cold and cruel defeat*
*Unable to offer a smile*
*Her crippled heart began to beat*
*And slowly all the while*

*She spread her wings and stood aright*
*Stared straight in soft blue eyes*
*In my dream I realized*
*I knew the swan some way*

*The Prince I knew a life gone by*
*A dreamy distant day*
*Dreamers know dreams are real*
*And life a fragile mirror*

*God is always helping*
*To reflect the image clear*
*And broken hearts can heal*
*When hope is truly real*

# *The Butterfly*

*Someone painted the sky today*
*The creamy clouds were whisked away*
*I asked a tree, "Were you the one?"*
*"Climbing and towering toward the sun?"*

*He quickly claimed in sad dismay*
*"Inquire the moon at break of day."*
*Impatiently, I bid "Adieu!"*
*And spotted a robin to seek a clue*

*Perched and puffed with pride he proclaimed*
*"I believe it was the soft still rain."*
*Unsatisfied, I slowly sighed when*
*My eyes alighted a butterfly*

*O creature of beauty, how could you know?*
*You flutter and fly too far below*
*He silently nestled near my ear*
*And whispered a secret soft and clear*

*"'Twas not the trees, nor moon, nor rain*
*And the robin exclaimed too quickly in vain*
*The trees were asleep and the rain was away*
*The moon humbly hid to see sun steal the day"*

*"I was the one so honored to view*
*'Twas God who painted the sky so blue*
*Careful and gentle and quiet was he*
*He grandly concluded and winked at me"*

*I captured his gaze, this creature so fair*
*Warming my heart he permitted a stare*
*The secret may spread to souls who believe*
*At the dawn of a day, God may be seen*

*Poems*

*By, Collin Wagner*

*The Seasons*
*The Staff*
*Long Nights*

# *Long Nights*

*Have no fear when you are alone,*
*When the cold wind chills to the bone.*
*Who you were before,*
*Does not matter anymore.*
*Today is a new day,*
*Let the Light shine your way.*

*You may feel you're falling,*
*When it is really your calling.*
*Remember the long nights of the past,*
*Remember all the questions you once asked.*
*The answer is there at the end of long night,*
*The answer reveals at the dawn's bright light.*

*Collin Wagner*

# *The Seasons*

*The seasons come, the seasons go,*
*Never forget them, for they always know.*
*The prayers of the kind, and the wishes of love,*
*For the light comes from within and above.*

*Down below, within the Earth,*
*A season to behold is of birth.*
*Remember the rites, at the right times,*
*Say the prayers, motions, feelings, and rhymes.*

*At the day of Yule, so it shall be,*
*Then shall come Imbolc for you and me.*
*Ostara of Spring, Beltane of May,*
*Litha of June, Lughnasadh on a hot Summer day.*

*Mabon of Autumn, the leaves will show,*
*Samhain of November, we all will know.*
*Know there is magic all around,*
*The earth's beauty will forever surround.*

*Collin Wagner*

# The Staff

The staff is tested, true and strong,
Let it take you places, let it tag along.

To save a fall, to help a rise,
To measure a mountain no matter the size.

For the staff is friend to those that wander,
Here, there, and ever yonder.

For the magician, sage, and everyone else,
The test of time, it has surely felt.

Never leave the staff behind,
For it is truly your friend, one of a kind.

*Collin Wagner*

# *Study Guide and Lesson Plans*

## *Questions for book club discussions and studies for children and adults*

1. *What examples from the stories reveal the themes of **friendship**?*

2. *What examples of characters from the stories are using **personification**? For example, what reveals the personification of the stars, willow tree, swan, and butterfly? What other examples can you find?*

3. *What are examples of **alliteration** and **rhyme scheme** from the stories?*

4. *In The Maiden's Journey, what are examples of **allusion** in the story? (One example is referring to a fairy tale.)*

5. *Explain the **mood** of each story! Do the moods change within each story? Are the moods happy, hopeful, sad, frightening? Do they inspire the reader? How does each story end in mood?*

6. *What are examples of **conflict** in each story? How does each conflict become resolved at the end?*

7. *Explain how the **mood, setting,** and elements of **fantasy** compare to classical fairy tales?*

## *Questions on the stories' genres*

1. *How can The Maiden's Journey be considered a literary **fantasy** or **fairy tale?***

2. *What are some **science fiction** elements in The Maiden's Journey?*

3. *Each story has magical events. Explain from each story the magical events and how it affects the **resolution.***

4. *What are examples of **adventure** and **suspense** in the stories?*

5. *What are examples of the beauty and power of **nature** in each story?*

## *Vocabulary*

*-Find 5 unfamiliar words or more from the stories and poems. Try to understand the meaning from context or use the dictionary to define.*

*Write the definition of each poetry term. You may use a dictionary or text book. Try to think of examples from the stories and poems.*

1. *Alliteration*
2. *Characterization*
3. *Conflict*
4. *Imagery*
5. *Metaphor*
6. *Mood*
7. *Onomatopoeia*
8. *Personification*
9. *Symbolism*
10. *Theme*

*Create a name to each of the following characters*

*-Mermaid*
*-Master/Angel*
*-Swan Princess*
*-Prince*
*-other swans*
*-the girl in The Butterfly*

### Creative activities for the classroom, home school, or book club

### Language Arts
-Create a scrapbook of favorite characters and/or elements of the story
-Research and present the stories of the Greek and Roman
gods of the sea, Neptune and Poseidon
-Write the story in prose

### Art
-Draw or paint the characters and/or the landscape of the story
-create a diorama or shadow box of the story

### Science
-Create a poster board or display board of the angel's and master's journey through space
-Write, present, an explanation of time, space, and the
cosmos, from the perspective of the story
-Create a hypothetical scientific formula to determine the
physics of the journey through the cosmos

### Mathematics
-Create a formula to calculate the time and distance of the journey of the maiden.

### Physical Education
-Plan and embark on a day's hike through locations similar to that of the story
-Spend a day in a pool, lake, or body of water experimenting
swimming and living as a sea creature
-create a dance to mirror the plot and mood of the story

### Music
-Create a song for the mermaid
-Choose a piece of music from the classical composers such as
Mozart, Bach, Tchaikovsky, for the theme song of the story
-Create an instrumental piece for the story

### History
-Research the history of mermaids
-Research the history of fairytales

*Note and Sketch page for your own ideas*

*Note and Sketch page for your own ideas*

*Write your own magical story or poem on this page!*

# *The Magical End*

*Contact Linda J. Wagner, Author*
*email readings@mysticalmagic.net*
*Facebook https://www.facebook.com/lindajwagnerauthor/*
*Website http://lindajwagnerauthor.net/*

Printed in the United States
By Bookmasters